RETURN TO THE
LIBRARY OF DOOM

INKFOOT

BY MICHAEL DAHL

ILLUSTRATED BY
BRADFORD KENDALL

ZONE BOOKS ARE PUBLISHED BY
STONE ARCH BOOKS
A CAPSTONE IMPRINT
151 GOOD COUNSEL DRIVE, P.O. BOX 669
MANKATO, MINNESOTA 56002
WWW.CAPSTONEPUB.COM

LIBRARY OF CONGRESS CATALOGING-IN-PUBLICATION DATA
IS AVAILABLE ON THE LIBRARY OF CONGRESS WEBSITE.

ISBN 978-1-4342-2146-9 (LIBRARY BINDING)

SUMMARY: THE LIBRARIAN HELPS OWEN DEFEAT THE LEGENDARY
INKFOOT.

ART DIRECTOR: KAY FRASER
GRAPHIC DESIGNER: HILARY WACHOLZ
PRODUCTION SPECIALIST: MICHELLE BIEDSCHEID

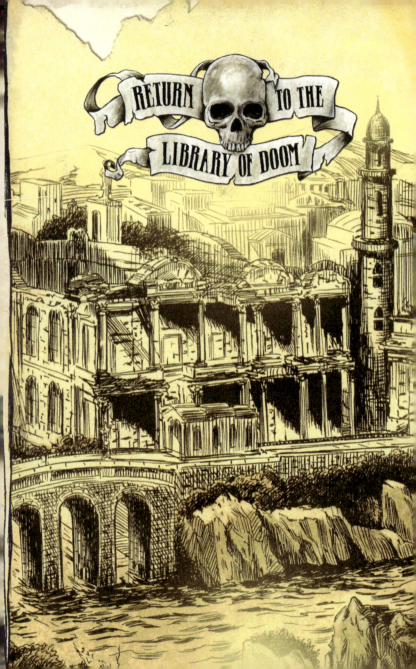

RETURN TO THE
LIBRARY OF DOOM

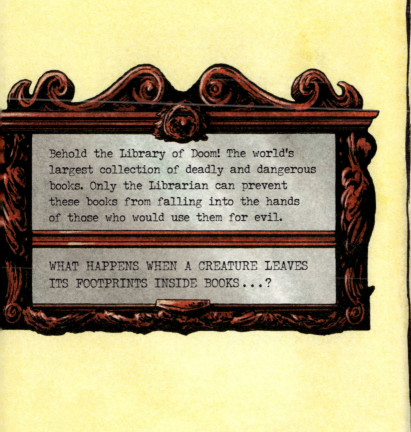

Behold the Library of Doom! The world's largest collection of deadly and dangerous books. Only the Librarian can prevent these books from falling into the hands of those who would use them for evil.

WHAT HAPPENS WHEN A CREATURE LEAVES ITS FOOTPRINTS INSIDE BOOKS...?

Chapter 1

WET

"What's wrong with Bronco?" asks

Owen's mother.

BRONCO is Owen's dog.

He has owned Bronco since the dog was a puppy.

Owen hears Bronco **growling** and barking outside.

"You better go bring him inside," says Owen's mother.

"Maybe he's got a **BEAR!**" says Owen's little brother, Doug.

Owen takes his flashlight and steps
outside.

Bronco has **STOPPED** barking.

"Where are you, boy?" calls Owen.

Owen's family lives in a town in the **MOUNTAINS**.

No one has ever seen a bear in the town before.

But Owen knows there is **ALWAYS** a first time.

Something big and dark crashes
through the bushes by the toolshed.

Owen sees another dark shape
LYING inside the toolshed.

"Bronco!" yells Owen.

The dog is quiet. It is still breathing, but its eyes are **SHUT**.

On the ground near Bronco's body are large **FOOTPRINTS**.

They are not bear prints. They are bigger than bear prints.

Owen also sees a book. It is an **overdue** library book.

He must have left it in the toolshed.

Owen knows he will have to **PAY** a huge fine.

Owen reaches out his hand to pet his injured dog.

The fur is wet. *Blood?* wonders Owen.

Owen **SHINES** his flashlight on his wet hand.

It is covered in thick black liquid.

INK.

Chapter 2
STRANGE SCRATCHES

Owen's mother called the vet after

Owen carried Bronco inside.

Owen and the vet both *LEAN* over the dog.

The vet wears gloves. He carefully checks Bronco's body.

"He's been scratched," says the vet. "It looks **BAD**."

Then the vet looks closely at
Bronco's eyes.

"I think your dog has been
poisoned," he says.

"Poison?" exclaims Owen's little
brother.

"I've never seen SCRATCHES like these before," says the vet. "I'm not sure what kind of animal attacked Bronco."

Then the vet looks at Owen's mother. "I think I should take the DOG back with me," he says.

The vet **drives** off with Bronco
in his back seat.

"Don't worry," says Owen's mother. "The vet will know what to do."

But *how could he?* wonders Owen. *He said he'd never seen scratches like that before.*

Who — or what — made those footprints?

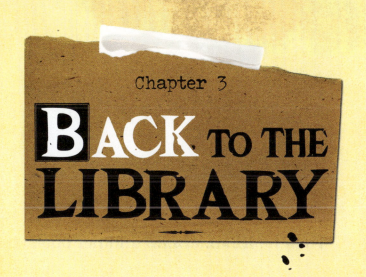

Chapter 3
BACK TO THE LIBRARY

Owen grabs his flashlight and steps back outside.

He **RETURNS** to the toolshed and picks up the library book. "This book is months overdue," he says to himself.

Owen doesn't have the money to pay the fine.

Then he **REMEMBERS** another book.

It was a book in the library that he loved to look through.

It had **PHOTOS** of every kind of animal's footprints.

Owen would be able to find the footprints of the animal that **HURT** his dog.

Then the vet would know how to treat Bronco. The boy glances quickly at his house.

Then he stuffs the book into his jacket pocket, and starts **running** down the road.

The woods are dark and cold.

Snowflakes fall from the frozen sky.

A few times, Owen hears growls

from behind the trees.

Each time he does, the library book

seems to **SQUIRM** in his pocket.

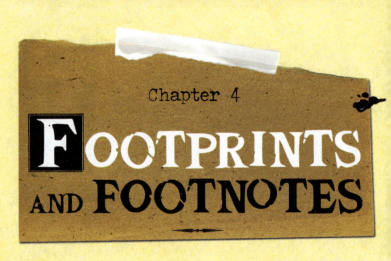

Chapter 4

FOOTPRINTS AND FOOTNOTES

Finally, Owen sees the light up ahead. He darts through the library door.

No one else is inside the library except for Ms. Eel.

"Almost **CLOSING** time, Owen,"
says Ms. Eel. "I'm getting ready to go
home."

"Yes, ma'am," says Owen.

He sets the overdue book on the
counter.

Then he **RUNS** toward a corner
of the library.

It is the reference section.

His eyes scan the titles of books on
animals and **HUNTING**.

"There's the book," whispers Owen.

He **PULLS** a thick book from the
top shelf.

The book is **FULL** of hundreds of photos.

Each photo shows an animal's footprints.

But something is **WRONG** with the book.

rooowwwggggg

Rrrwwwooggglllllll   4 Hrroogh   5

Yaaauuuuuugggghhh   7 Aaaawwwrrggghhh

Yyeeeaaauuuwawaaa 10 Sssccrrnneeeceee

3 Uuooogghhhlaaa   14 Sshhraaaaekaka www 18

16 Jrawwwwlloob 17 Aaawwwrrgghh   20 Hrrrrggh

19 Grrrooowwwggggg   23 RRrrwwwwooggll

22 OooAaaauugghhh   27 Grrrooowww

26 Yaaauuuuugggghhh   29 Yyeeeaaauuuwa

28 Wooupeergggghhh   31 RRrrooorrg

RRrrwwwwooggglHHHl   33 RRrrwwwwoog

RRrrccrnneeecceee   36 Sshhraaaae

35 Uuooogghhhlaaa   39 Jrawwwa

38 Hrrrrrrooughh   42 Hrrr

41 Sshhraaaaekakawww   45 Grooooohhhh

44 Hrroogh   45   49 Yyeeeaa

48 Waauuugghhh   52 Hrrrr

51 Grooooohhhhllll   56 Yaaauu

The 55 Waauuugghhh   59 Sssctt

58 Ooraauugah   62

61 YYaaauuuugggghhh

On page after page, the **PHOTOS** are covered up.

Some are crowded off the page.

The book has been filled with strange **FOOTNOTES**.

41 wwwwwwahhhhh

56 gggggrrrrrrrrwwwwww

Owen **FLIPS** through more and
more pages.

He can't find the footprints he is
looking for.

Ms. Eel steps into the aisle.

"Owen," she says, "did you know there's a **BIG** fine on that book you brought back?"

Then she looks over the boy's shoulder and sees the reference book.

Ms. Eel gasps. "Not again!" she whispers.

Chapter 5

THE LEGEND

Owen watches Ms. Eel's eyes

GROW wide with fear.

Ms. Eel suddenly pulls another book off the shelf and **OPENS** it.

Then she grabs another and another. She opens each book and **THROWS** it to the floor.

Then Ms. Eel glances around the empty library. "We have to get out of here," she says.

"What's going on?" asks Owen.

"It's here again," says Ms. Eel. "We have to leave. NOW!"

"What's here?" asks Owen. He hears a loud growl outside the library door.

Ms. Eel freezes.

Then she grabs Owen's hand. "In the back room," she says. "Hurry!"

The growl **GROWS** louder.

Suddenly, several books fly off the shelves.

Ms. Eel **SCREAMS** and covers her head.

Owen and Ms. Eel run into the back room of the library. She quickly **TURNS** and locks the door behind them.

The woman stares **nervously** through a small window in the door.

"What's going on?" demands Owen. "And what's wrong with all the books?"

Ms. Eel kneels down. "Have you ever heard of **INKFOOT?**" she asks quietly.

Owen frowns. "You mean Bigfoot?" he asks.

"No, Inkfoot," says Ms. Eel. "Bigfoot is just a myth. Inkfoot is real."

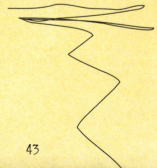

"He **HIDES** inside books," explains Ms. Eel. "Most people never know he even exists, until he comes out of the books. And he never does that unless something makes him **ANGRY**. Or frightens him."

Like a barking dog? Owen thinks to himself.

Ms. Eel grabs the book that Owen was still holding.

"See these pages?" she says. "Footnotes. That's how you **FOLLOW** his trail."

Owen stares down at the pages.

He looks at the footnotes covering

the photos.

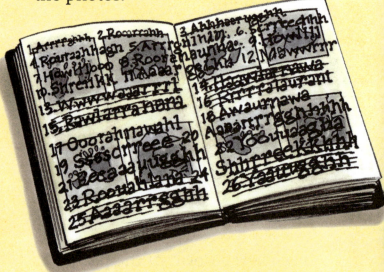

He thinks of the **INK** that

covered Bronco's fur.

Owen needs to tell the vet about Inkfoot.

"We have to call for **HELP**," he says.

"There's no phone back here," says Ms. Eel. "I don't have a cell phone with me. Do you?"

Owen shakes his head.

Owen stands up and looks out through the door's **WINDOW.**

Facing the window is a tall shelf of books.

In the spines of the books, Owen sees a **dark** shape.

The shadow stretches from the bottom shelf all the way to the top.

The shadow seems to cover at least a hundred books.

It looks like a gigantic **hairy** beast.

Chapter 6

INKFOOT

"It's out there," says Owen.

The creature's growls fill the library.

Shadowy arms throw books and shelves to the floor.

They **hurl** chairs against tables.

Hairy fists **smash** through computer screens.

"I can't see it now," says the boy.

Then he looks down at the floor of the library's main room.

A **DARK** puddle covers the rug.

The puddle is GROWING.

"Owen!" yells Ms. Eel. "Look!"

Ink is **seeping** through the bottom of the door.

Soon, the ink is several feet deep. The thick, dark liquid **SWIRLS** through the room.

"Don't touch it," says Owen. "It's poison!"

Owen looks at Ms. Eel. She is touching a shiny brooch pinned to her sweater.

It is shaped like the letter L. The L begins to **GLOW**.

A **WHIRLPOOL** forms in the middle of the room.

The ink begins to drain away, pouring down the sides of a huge well.

Suddenly, a man **FLIES** up from the well.

He wears a long **dark** coat and dark glasses.

"The Librarian!" shouts Ms. Eel.

"I came as soon as I saw your signal," says the man, nodding at her **BROOCH**.

He flies out the door of the back room and into the library.

The shadow of Inkfoot rises up among the bookshelves.

The Librarian raises his hands. A powerful wind blows from his fingertips.

The monster's shadow **BREAKS** into small, square pieces.

"Here is Inkfoot," says the man.
"Or, at least what's left of him."

The Librarian shows a piece of
paper to Ms. Eel. It is a sheet of
ENDNOTES.

Then the wind blows Owen's
overdue book into the Librarian's
hands.

The **man** looks down at it and grins.

"If you don't mind, Ms. Eel," says the Librarian. "Instead of being **OVERDUE**, I think what we need is a do over."

The man **claps** the covers of the book together.

A blaze of lightning **FLASHES** through the library.

Owen and Ms. Eel both gasp. The library has been **returned** to normal.

All the books are back in their place. The computers and chairs are no longer **smashed**.

Ms. Eel looks up at the clock. "Closing time," she says.

She tells Owen NOT to worry about the fine.

And when Owen **RUSHES** back home, a healthy Bronco runs out to greet him.

Author

Michael Dahl is the author of more than 200 books for children and young adults. He has won the AEP Distinguished Achievement Award three times for his nonfiction. His Finnegan Zwake mystery series was shortlisted twice by the Anthony and Agatha awards. He has also written the Library of Doom series. He is a featured speaker at conferences around the country on graphic novels and high-interest books for boys.

Illustrator

Bradford Kendall has enjoyed drawing for as long as he can remember. As a boy, he loved to read comic books and watch old monster movies. He graduated from Rhode Island School of Design with a BFA in Illustration. He has owned his own commercial art business since 1983, and lives in Providence, Rhode Island, with his wife, Leigh, and their two children Lily and Stephen. They also have a cat named Hansel and a dog named Gretel.

GLOSSARY

brooch (BROOCH or BROHCH)—a piece of jewelry that can be pinned to your clothes

fine (FINE)—a sum of money paid as punishment for doing something wrong

footnote (FUT-noht)—a note at the bottom of a page that explains something in the text. Endnotes are the same notes, but collected at the end of a chapter or a book.

injured (IN-jurd)—hurt

myth (MITH)—a story that people believe

overdue (oh-vur-DOO)—late

poisoned (POI-zuhnd)—given a harmful substance

reference (REF-uh-ruhnss)—a book that helps find information

scan (SKAN)—look carefully and closely

signal (SIG-nuhl)—a way of sending a message

spines (SPINEZ)—the central, vertical pieces of book covers

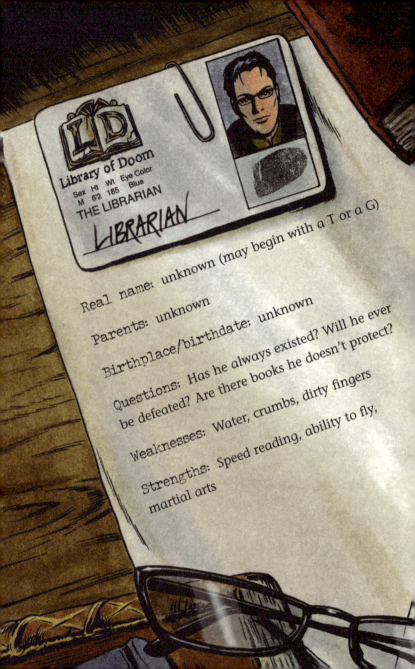

Library of Doom

Sex	Ht	Wt	Eye Color
M	6'2	185	Blue

THE LIBRARIAN

LIBRARIAN

Real name: unknown (may begin with a T or a G)

Parents: unknown

Birthplace/birthdate: unknown

Questions: Has he always existed? Will he ever be defeated? Are there books he doesn't protect?

Weaknesses: Water, crumbs, dirty fingers

Strengths: Speed reading, ability to fly, martial arts

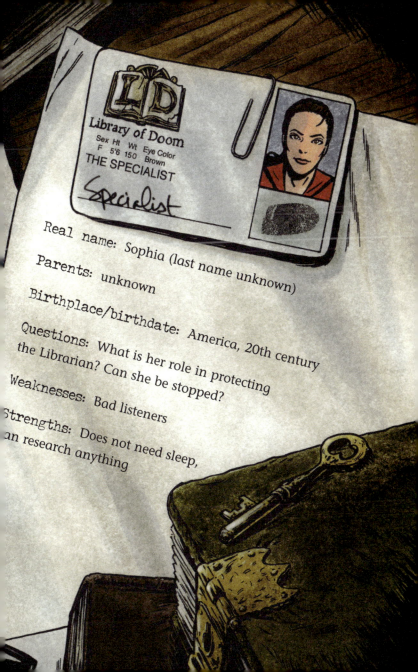

Library of Doom

Sex F Ht 5'6 Wt 150 Eye Color Brown

THE SPECIALIST

Specialist

Real name: Sophia (last name unknown)

Parents: unknown

Birthplace/birthdate: America, 20th century

Questions: What is her role in protecting the Librarian? Can she be stopped?

Weaknesses: Bad listeners

Strengths: Does not need sleep, can research anything

INKFOOT

After leaving Ms. Eel's library, the Librarian took the piece of paper containing Inkfoot's endnotes to the Specialist's lab. There, the Specialist tested the paper. Using a special kind of disappearing ink, she tried to erase the Inkfoot endnotes. It did not work.

She then tried to burn the paper. It burned, but the notes collected on a nearby notepad.

When the Specialist tried to destroy the notepad by cutting it into tiny pieces of paper, the notepad turned into a small pack of sticky notes.

They now remain in the Librarian's office, locked safely away.

DISCUSSION QUESTIONS

1. Is it fair for a librarian to fine a student who does not **return** a book on time? Why or why not?

2. If Owen had not gone to the library, what do you think would have **HAPPENED**?

3. Owen goes to the library to figure out what kind of animal could have attacked his dog. What would you have done?

WRITING PROMPTS

1. Imagine another way that the Librarian could have defeated **INKFOOT**. How does he do it? Write about it.

2. **CREATE** your own book cover. Don't forget to add the text on the back and give your book a title!

3. Write about your favorite book. What is it about? Who wrote it? Why is it your favorite?